ANIMAL ALPHABET

BERT KITCHEN

for Corinna and Saskia

PATRICK HARDY BOOKS

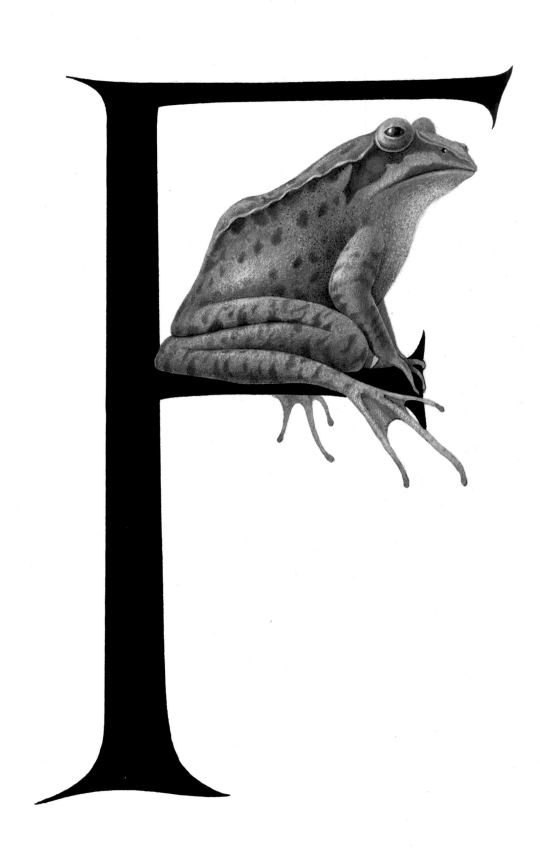

ANIMAL ANSWERS

A	Armadillo (Nine-banded)	**N**	Newt
B	Bat	**O**	Ostrich
C	Chameleon (Mediterranean)	**P**	Penguin (Rockhopper)
D	Dodo	**Q**	Quetzal
E	Elephant	**R**	Rhinoceros
F	Frog	**S**	Snail
G	Giraffe	**T**	Tortoise
H	Hedgehog	**U**	Umbrella Bird
I	Iguana	**V**	Vulture (Ruppell's)
J	Jerboa	**W**	Walrus
K	Koala	**X**	X-ray Fish (Pristella riddlei)
L	Lion	**Y**	Yak
M	Magpie (Pica pica) and Mole	**Z**	Zebra (chapman's)

PATRICK HARDY BOOKS
28 Percy Street,
London WIP 9FF, UK.

First published in 1984

ISBN 0 7444 0024 4

Printed in Italy

108705